MW01001128

April & Mae

and the

Animal Shelter

EVERY DAY
WITH
April & Mae

SUNDAY

MONDAY

TUESDAY

WEDNESDAY

THURSDAY

FRIDAY

SATURDAY

Collect them ALL!

April & Mae

and the

Animal Shelter

THE THURSDAY BOOK

MEGAN DOWD LAMBERT

Illustrated by BRIANA DENGOUE

i◠i Charlesbridge

To my daughter Caroline, who loves animals
and is a good friend. I love you and am so lucky
to be your mom.—M. D. L.

To my daughter, Bellarose.—B. D.

Text copyright © 2023 by Megan Dowd Lambert
Illustrations copyright © 2023 by Briana Arrington-Dengoue
All rights reserved, including the right of reproduction in whole
or in part in any form. Charlesbridge and colophon are registered
trademarks of Charlesbridge Publishing, Inc.

At the time of publication, all URLs printed in this book were accurate
and active. Charlesbridge, the author, and the illustrator are not responsible
for the content or accessibility of any website.

Published by Charlesbridge
9 Galen Street, Watertown, MA 02472 • (617) 926-0329 • www.charlesbridge.com

Library of Congress Cataloging-in-Publication Data
Names: Lambert, Megan Dowd, author. | Dengoue, Briana, illustrator.
Title: April & Mae and the animal shelter: the Thursday book /
    Megan Dowd Lambert; illustrated by Briana Dengoue.
Other titles: April and Mae and the animal shelter
Description: Watertown, MA: Charlesbridge, [2023] | Series: Every day with
    April & Mae | Audience: Ages 5–8. | Summary: "April and Mae are best friends
    (and so are their pets). When they decide to help the new animal shelter with
    their own talents, Mae raises money to buy cat food with a lemonade stand and
    April writes a letter to the newspaper to encourage animal rescue."—Provided
    by publisher.
Identifiers: LCCN 2021028998 (print) | LCCN 2021028999 (ebook) |
    ISBN 9781623542627 (hardcover) | ISBN 9781632898548 (ebook)
Subjects: LCSH: Best friends—Juvenile fiction. | Friendship—Juvenile fiction. |
    Animal shelters—Juvenile fiction. | Voluntarism—Juvenile fiction. | CYAC:
    Best friends—Fiction. | Friendship—Fiction. | Animal shelters—Fiction. |
    Voluntarism—Fiction.
Classification: LCC PZ7.1.L26 Ai 2023 (print) | LCC PZ7.1.L26 (ebook) |
    DDC 813.6 [E]—dc23
LC record available at https://lccn.loc.gov/2021028998
LC ebook record available at https://lccn.loc.gov/2021028999

Printed in China
(hc) 10 9 8 7 6 5 4 3 2 1

Illustrations done in Photoshop
Illustrations line art finalized by Gisela Bohórquez
Illustrations colorized by Collaborate
Display type set in Jacoby by Adobe
Text type set in Grenadine by Markanna Studios Inc.
Printed by 1010 Printing International Limited in Huizhou, Guangdong, China
Production supervision by Jennifer Most Delaney
Designed by Cathleen Schaad

April and Mae
want to help
the new animal shelter.

April likes to use
her words to help.
Mae likes to use
her hands to help.
Mae wants to help cats.
April wants to help dogs.

But April and Mae are friends.
Best friends.
And their pets
are best friends, too.

One Thursday,
Mae sets up
a lemonade stand.
She squeezes lemons.
She pours water.
She mixes in sugar.
She adds sprigs of mint.

Mae will sell lemonade.
The money she makes
will buy cat food
for the animal shelter.
She wonders
if she made enough.

The same Thursday,
April decides to write
a letter to the newspaper.
Her letter will ask
people to get a dog from
the animal shelter.
"Every dog needs a home,"
writes April.

Mae sells lots of lemonade.
She puts the money
in a big jar.

LEMONADE

$ 1.00 a cup

She is glad!
"I can buy so much cat food!"
says Mae.

April sits at her desk.
She looks at her pen.
Her dog rubs his head
on her leg.
April does not know
what else to write.
She wonders what words
can help find *all*
the dogs homes.

April hears a knock
at her door.
It is Mae and her cat.
The friends hug.

"What is in that big jar?" asks April.

"Money from my lemonade stand," says Mae.

"I love lemonade!" says April.

"I saved some for you," says Mae.

"Thanks," says April.

"You're welcome," says Mae.

"Is there more?" asks April.
"No. I sold the lemonade.
Now I have money.
I will buy cat food for the
animal shelter," says Mae.
"That is a good way
to help," says April.

"What are you doing today?"
asks Mae.
"I want to write a letter
to the newspaper," says April.
"What is the letter about?" asks Mae.
"It is about the animal shelter.
It says every dog
needs a home," says April.
"That is a good way
to help," says Mae.

"But it is hard to write my letter,"
 says April.
"Why?" asks Mae.
"I feel so sad about *all* the
 dogs without homes," says April.

"Yes. I feel sad about
cats without food, too," says Mae.

"One letter is not enough
to help *all* the dogs," says April.

"One letter is like
  one cup of lemonade,"
  says Mae.
"How?" asks April.

"The first cup I sold
 was not enough
 to buy lots of cat food,"
 says Mae.
"No," says April.
"But bit by bit
 I sold lots of cups," says Mae.
"And now you can buy
 lots of cat food?" asks April.
"Yes!" says Mae.

"Maybe one letter will help
   one dog find a home," says April.
"Yes," says Mae.
"And I can write
   more letters," says April.
"More letters can help
   more dogs," says Mae.

The friends hug.

April works on her letter.
Mae counts the money
in her jar.

"I am ready to mail my letter," says April.

"I am ready to buy cat food," says Mae.

April mails her letter.
Mae buys cat food.

CAT FOOD
$

Then the friends and their pets
go to the animal shelter.

The people at the animal shelter
are happy to get the cat food.
They are happy to hear
about April's letter, too.
They ask April and Mae,
"Do you want to walk the dogs?
Do you want to pet the cats?"

"Yes!" says April.

"Yes!" says Mae.

The friends are glad
for more ways to help.

When April and Mae leave,
the people at the shelter
say, "Come back soon."
"We will!"
say April and Mae.
"Woof!" says April's dog.
"Meow!" says Mae's cat.

The friends walk home.
"It feels good to do good,"
says April.
"It feels good to do good
with a good friend," says Mae.
"A *best* friend," says April.

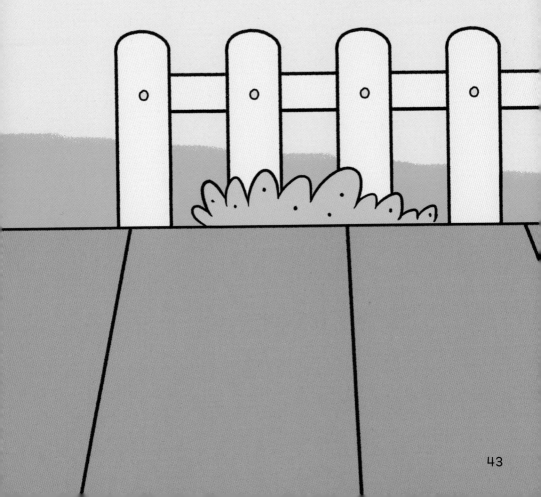

April and Mae smile.
"We can help
 bit by bit," says April.
"Bit by bit," says Mae.
"With our words
 and our hands," says April.
"And our hearts," says Mae.
"That is enough," says April.
"It is," says Mae.

The friends hug.

"Goodbye, April," says Mae.
"Goodbye, Mae," says April.

And goodbye to you.
Can you think of
ways to help, too?